WHITE MONKEY

WHITE MONKEY

Mark Will

CADMUS & HARMONY MEDIA

CADMUS & HARMONY MEDIA

CADMUS & HARMONY MEDIA:
http://facebook.com/cadmus.harmony.media
http://twitter.com/CadmusHarmony
http://instagram.com/cadmusharmony

MARK WILL:
http://facebook.com/mark.will.write
http://twitter.com/MarkWillWrite
http://instagram.com/markwillwrite
http://goodreads.com/markwillwrite
http://amazon.com/author/markwill

WHITE MONKEY

NOTE

White Monkey was originally conceived as a screenplay but may easily be reimagined for the stage. Those with dramaturgical rather than cinematic predilections are encouraged to ignore all references to framing, fades, titles, subtitles, and credit rolls and to substitute the strategic use of spotlights for cuts. In actuality, however, this work is not intended to be filmed or performed. It exists only in the mind of the reader.

WHITE MONKEY

Black screen. Title in white text: WHITE MONKEY. Black screen. Face of WHITE MONKEY—of pithecanthropic aspect, with white makeup, large white teeth, red lips, black eyeliner—appears as if illuminated by flashlight. INTERROGATOR, off-screen, asks WHITE MONKEY questions in English, which he answers in English. All dialogue appears in white Chinese subtitles, with INTERROGATOR's lines in column on left and WHITE MONKEY's on right.

INTERROGATOR

Name.

WHITE MONKEY

What?

INTERROGATOR

Name.

WHITE MONKEY

White Monkey.

INTERROGATOR

What?

WHITE MONKEY

What?

INTERROGATOR

What did you say?

WHITE MONKEY

I said White Monkey.

INTERROGATOR

No.

WHITE MONKEY

Yes.

INTERROGATOR

What is your name?

WHITE MONKEY

My name is White Monkey.

INTERROGATOR

That is not your name. What is your real name?

WHITE MONKEY

My real name is White Monkey.

INTERROGATOR

No.

WHITE MONKEY

Yes.

INTERROGATOR

What do you mean?

WHITE MONKEY

What do you mean?

INTERROGATOR

You must give your real name.

WHITE MONKEY

I give you the name you gave me.

INTERROGATOR

The name who gave you?

WHITE MONKEY

The name you gave me.

INTERROGATOR

Who?

WHITE MONKEY

You.

INTERROGATOR

What are you talking about?

WHITE MONKEY

I'm talking about you. You singular and you plural. Is there really a difference, so far as you are concerned? Do you singular have a mind of your own? Or are you merely a reflection of you plural?

INTERROGATOR

You are being impertinent. What is your real name? It must be written down.

WHITE MONKEY

Why do you use the passive voice?

INTERROGATOR

What are you saying?

WHITE MONKEY

I'm saying that by using the passive voice you may be trying to obscure the fact that there is an agent who will perform the act of writing. Perhaps you are hoping to avoid personal responsibility for the writing which you yourself will do when you write down my name.

INTERROGATOR

You are being impertinent. What is your real name?

WHITE MONKEY

My real name is White Monkey. Write it down.

INTERROGATOR

That name is not permitted. It is not your real name.

WHITE MONKEY

You know very well that at this particular time and in this particular place it is the realest name I have. It is the name you gave me. What is more real than that?

INTERROGATOR

That name is not allowed.

WHITE MONKEY

Not allowed by whom? By you individually or by the plurality which you as an individual represent? To whom am I speaking? Are you an autonomous person?

Or are you merely the mouthpiece of a nation, a culture, an ethnicity?

INTERROGATOR

You are being impertinent. What is your real name?

WHITE MONKEY

What does it matter if I tell you my name is Mike Smith or Kevin Jones or Ryan Wilson or Tim Greene? To you my name will always be White Monkey.

INTERROGATOR

That name is not allowed. Your real name must be written down on an official document.

WHITE MONKEY

Then write down White Monkey and make it official. You brought me to your country as a rare and exotic species. I came willingly, I admit, to entertain you and your children. Your newly constructed zoo is a marvel. I am well fed. At night I am allowed to return to my private lodgings, which have all the modern amenities. You look the other way when I frolic with your women. I am, to some extent, a creature of privilege. And, although they too are granted certain indulgences, I know that I am better treated than my colleagues Black Monkey, Brown Monkey, and even Yellow Monkey. But during the day, when I am locked inside my cage, I understand clearly what my true identity here is. Until you acknowledge my human qualities, I will insist on being called White Monkey. Write it down.

INTERROGATOR

That may not be written on an official document because it is not your real name.

WHITE MONKEY

Your bureaucratized brain refuses to see that we are related, that we are in fact brothers. You and I are imprisoned by the same authoritarian system. Why should we be enemies, rather than allies in revolt against the forces which oppress us both? Don't you see that there is a choice?

INTERROGATOR

You are being impertinent. What is your real name?

WHITE MONKEY

I have studied your philosophers. I have experienced awe in the presence of your cultural and natural wonders.

I have eaten your food with gusto. I have burned incense for your gods. Is there no common ground between us?

INTERROGATOR

You must give your real name.

WHITE MONKEY

I have celebrated your land and your people in song. I have commemorated your nation in art of idiosyncratic beauty. Your own myths and legends revere my simian predecessor as a hero. Until you recognize me as something other than a contemptible alien, I will insist that you call me White Monkey. Write it down.

INTERROGATOR

That may not be written on an official document. What is your real name?

WHITE MONKEY

You expect deference and respect, yet you give none in return. You contradict your own cherished principles in your dealings with me. How can there be harmony between us? How can there be a balance of opposites? How can there be fairness or justice? Until you demonstrate an understanding of the concept of reciprocality, I will insist that you call me by the name you gave me: White Monkey.

INTERROGATOR

You must give your real name.

WHITE MONKEY

By real name do you mean the name my mother gave me? What do you care about my mother? Her name was White Monkey. My father's name was White Monkey. I, their son, am White Monkey. That is my name. Write it down.

INTERROGATOR

That is not your name. Your real name must be written on an official document which is to be stamped by the Higher Authority.

WHITE MONKEY

What authority is higher than the Self? I myself tell you that my real name, my actual name, my official name is White Monkey, the name that you gave me, the emblem of your bigotry. Write it down.

INTERROGATOR

I cannot write that name on an official document.

WHITE MONKEY

And so the mask is removed. You said I. First person singular. There is an ego behind that voice after all. Is it possible that you are not a robot, not a mechanized android?

Cut to INTERROGATOR, who appears as if illuminated by flashlight, covering his face with his hands. WHITE MONKEY is off-screen.

INTERROGATOR

You are being impertinent. Tell me your real name.

WHITE MONKEY

Do you have feelings too? Are you able to cry? Do you bleed when you are stabbed? My name is White Monkey. Write it down.

INTERROGATOR

No. I cannot write that name down. I will not.

WHITE MONKEY

Then write this down: Fuck Your Mother.

INTERROGATOR

No. Don't speak that way. You are being very impertinent.

WHITE MONKEY

I was just expressing for your mother the same concern you have for mine. Are you bleeding now? Are you crying?

INTERROGATOR

You are being very impertinent indeed. I can no longer assist you. Your case is being transferred to the Higher Authority.

WHITE MONKEY

I told you already that there is no authority higher than the Self.

Fade to black.

WHITE MONKEY

Where did he go? Was I too harsh? I was only joking, wasn't I? Or was I? I just wanted to make a point, to establish a philosophical premise. What else could I do but try to jolt him into awareness?

Face of WHITE MONKEY appears as if illuminated by flashlight. INTERROGATOR is off-screen.

INTERROGATOR

Name.

WHITE MONKEY

What?

INTERROGATOR

Name.

WHITE MONKEY

This again? My name is White Monkey. Who are you?

INTERROGATOR

I am a representative of the Higher Authority, Plenipotentiary of Official Documents, Custodian of the Executive Stamp.

WHITE MONKEY

That's very impressive. But if what you say is true, why does your voice sound exactly like your alleged subordinate's?

INTERROGATOR

A coincidence and nothing more. Now please give me your real name so that I may write it down on an official document and stamp it.

WHITE MONKEY

I told you my name is White Monkey.

INTERROGATOR

And I told you to give me your real name.

WHITE MONKEY

My real name is White Monkey.

INTERROGATOR

You know that's not true. The Committee has been very patient with you thus far, in spite of your impertinence, but we now demand that you give us your real name.

WHITE MONKEY

And so the mask is reassumed. You said We. First person plural. The individual will has once again been absorbed by the collective.

Cut to INTERROGATOR, who appears as if illuminated by flashlight—incorporeal, iconic, a disk like the sun, blue, with white rays around the circumference and the word "LIE" in white in the center.

INTERROGATOR

Your interpretations of these circumstances are irrelevant to the Committee. The fact remains that you must give us your real name so that it may be written down on an official document which is to be stamped. If you are unwilling to cooperate, we have ways of compelling you.

Cut to WHITE MONKEY.

WHITE MONKEY

Coward. Show your face so I can spit in it.

Cut to INTERROGATOR.

INTERROGATOR

Don't be vulgar. Your insults will profit you nothing. Don't you know the extent of our power and influence? We control everything and everyone. We own everything and everyone. We own the zoo where you work. We own your zoomaster, who is greatly indebted to us. And we own you too. Now tell us your real name.

Cut to WHITE MONKEY.

WHITE MONKEY

My real name is White Monkey. Write it down.

Cut to INTERROGATOR.

INTERROGATOR

You are wasting time.

Cut to WHITE MONKEY.

WHITE MONKEY

Then write this down: Fuck Your Mother.

Cut to INTERROGATOR.

INTERROGATOR

That jest was merely insipid the first time you made it.
Now it has become tediously offensive. Tell us your real
name.

Cut to WHITE MONKEY.

WHITE MONKEY

Why should I give you a name other than the one you
gave me?

Cut to INTERROGATOR.

INTERROGATOR

Because if you don't, we will crush you, just like we crushed all the other White Monkeys before you, and all the Black Monkeys, and all the Brown Monkeys, and all the Yellow Monkeys—especially the Yellow Monkeys.

Cut to WHITE MONKEY.

WHITE MONKEY

So you admit that my name is White Monkey?

Cut to INTERROGATOR.

INTERROGATOR

We admit nothing. If you like, we can agree that, so far as we are concerned, you are nothing but a pasty-faced ape, an unwelcome outlander, a subhuman barbarian unworthy of any consideration or respect. But we will never write this on an official document which is to be stamped.

Cut to WHITE MONKEY.

WHITE MONKEY

And why not?

Cut to INTERROGATOR.

INTERROGATOR

Let's just say it would be bad for business.

Cut to WHITE MONKEY.

WHITE MONKEY

Your committee is a conspiracy of villains. I will advertise your crimes. The public will learn the truth. They will rise up. They will protest the injustice.

Cut to INTERROGATOR.

INTERROGATOR

Who will? The other animals in the zoo? The so-called opposition party, which is really just an extension of our own? The leaders of the country which you abandoned to come here? By tomorrow your story will be completely forgotten. Did we not just tell you that we own everything and everyone? We make the laws and appoint the judges. We control the newspapers and the television stations. Nobody will even know what happened to you. You will be disappeared, erased from existence, deleted from history. And we, the members of the Committee, will sleep soundly as ever, knowing that we protected the status quo from a foreign pestilence and rid ourselves of a bestial annoyance.

Cut to WHITE MONKEY, who is silent.

Cut to INTERROGATOR.

INTERROGATOR

Yes, it seems that you are finally ready to cooperate. Now tell us your real name.

Cut to WHITE MONKEY.

WHITE MONKEY

My real name is White Monkey.

Cut to INTERROGATOR.

INTERROGATOR

What do you hope to achieve with your martyrdom? You yourself have admitted that within certain limits you enjoy a life of privilege here. Do you really want to give it all up over a name? What's in a name? To paraphrase the great poet of your language, a monkey by any other name will still stink. The Committee is quite willing to forgive you for your impertinence. If you sign your real name to a letter of apology which we will publicize through our media sources, we will allow you to return to your job at the zoo with full benefits. We have already made the arrangements with your zoomaster, our faithful servant. Now, for the last time, what is your name, your real name, your actual name, your official name?

Cut to WHITE MONKEY.

WHITE MONKEY

My name is White Monkey. Write it down, motherfucker.

Cut to INTERROGATOR, who now appears as a gun pointed directly at WHITE MONKEY and/or the audience.

INTERROGATOR

Behold the true face of the Committee. In spite of your sins, we forgive you, for you know not what you do.

INTERROGATOR fires gun. Fade to white. Roll credits in black text.

LIE

ABOUT THE AUTHOR

MARK WILL is a writer in permanent exile. Currently based on the island of Taiwan, he is the editor-in-chief of the independent imprint Cadmus & Harmony Media. His latest publication is the story collection *Jigs & Tales of Bawdry*. Will is also the songwriter, vocalist, and bassist of the musical collective [ai], whose new album *Carmina Formosa Deluxe* is available from Amazon, iTunes, and other digital retailers. Despite his professed aversion to social media, Will may be found on Facebook, Twitter, and Instagram.

ALSO FROM CADMUS & HARMONY MEDIA

Of Letters and a Man: A
by Mark Will

The first canto of Mark Will's projected 26-canto epic.

Amazon:

"truly the work of an alchemist"

"superbly ambitious and skillfully executed"

"clearly the rich work of a craftsman who understands
his chosen medium"

Audible:

"a rare jewel in contemporary poetry"

"Guy Bethell performs the poems beautifully and evokes
a Shakespearean mood."

Message
by Fernando Pessoa
translated by Mark Will

Mark Will's new unabridged translation of the great modern epic of Portugal.

Amazon:

"This wonderful English translation of Pessoa's *Mensagem* is for me an insight into the once great seafaring nation."

Audible:

"Another excellent performance by Guy Bethell. His dulcet voice delivers with a poise and grace which reveals and clarifies esoteric elements of the book."

Persians
by Aeschylus
translated by Mark Will

Mark Will's new translation of Aeschylus' historical tragedy with preface, notes, maps, and timelines.

Amazon:

"a literal translation that retains the poetry of the original Greek"

Audible:

"an ancient classic that remains relevant today"

Flannsday
by Mark Will & G.J. Villa

The first novelette in the *Erinesque* series introduces readers to Martin Wells and J.G. Vara on day one of their quixotic "literary wank" across Ireland.

Amazon:

"a fun, playful and hilarious story"

"a book of many references, an irreverent sense of humor, and much wit, all contained in a very efficiently-worded package"

Jigs & Tales of Bawdry
by Mark Will

Mark Will's first collection of short fiction is an irreverent commentary on contemporary American life, from the Reagan era to the post-9/11 present.

Amazon:

"these Bukowski-esque shorts may offend a few readers"

"light and dark, comedy and pathos"

Thank you for reading *White Monkey*. If you enjoyed this work, please leave a review at Amazon, Goodreads, or wherever literature is discussed online.

CADMUS & HARMONY MEDIA